www.raintreepublishers.co.uk
Visit our website to find out
more information about
Raintree books.

To order:
☎ Phone 0845 6044371
📄 Fax +44 (0) 1865 312263
✉ Email myorders@raintreepublishers.co.uk

Customers from outside the UK please telephone +44 1865 312262

Raintree is an imprint of Capstone Global Library Limited,
a company incorporated in England and Wales having its
registered office at 7 Pilgrim Street, London, EC4V 6LB –
Registered company number: 6695582

First published by Stone Arch Books in 2011
First published in the United Kingdom in 2012
The moral rights of the proprietor have been asserted.

Art Director: Bob Lentz
Designer: Brann Garvey
Production Specialist: Michelle Biedscheid
Editor: Diyan Leake
Originated by Capstone Global Library Ltd
Printed and bound in China by Leo Paper Products Ltd

ISBN 978 1 406 23688 0
16 15 14 13 12 11
10 9 8 7 6 5 4 3 2 1

British Library Cataloguing in Publication Data
A full catalogue record for this book is available from the

CONTENTS

CHAPTER 1

KING KALEIDOSCOPE

It was a quiet summer Saturday in Central City. The morning rain had tapered off. Now the sun was out, shining through the moisture in the air.

Police scientist Barry Allen glanced up at the sky. He cautiously drove his car along Route 74 towards S.T.A.R. Labs' Central City location. In the distance, a rainbow arched across the horizon.

"I'll have to tell Iris about that," Barry said to himself.

His wife loved rainbows and always pointed them out when she saw them. Maybe if he told Iris, she wouldn't be so annoyed that he was late to meet her once again. Despite being the Flash, the World's Fastest Man, Barry was often running behind schedule.

A few blocks from his destination, Barry pulled up at some traffic lights and sighed. Iris was very excited about the King Kaleidoscope demonstration at S.T.A.R. Labs. The kaleidoscope had been designed by the high-tech laboratory to showcase their new light-projection technology, as well as other scientific advances. Most of the city's celebrities were going to be there.

Iris had reminded Barry several times to meet her at exactly noon. He looked at his watch. It was already 12.15.

Barry had just come from the crime lab where he'd been analysing some important evidence. As usual, he had lost track of the time.

In the S.T.A.R. Labs parking lot, Barry found an empty spot and then hurried into the building. He headed towards the giant atrium in the heart of the complex.

The courtyard was full of people. They were milling around a huge metallic tube in the centre of the room. Even with the air conditioning on, the atrium was warm from the sun streaming through the glass skylight above.

Barry scanned the crowd for Iris. He quickly spotted the mayor, with his wife and kids, near a bunch of bigwig businessmen and the chief of police.

He also recognized the star quarterback of the Cougars, Central City's football team, along with a local news reader and beauty queen. Everyone had brought their families and friends. Then finally, Barry spotted Iris standing beside a potted palm. Iris smiled at him and waved.

"Sorry," Barry told his wife, hurrying to her side.

"You mean about being late?" Iris asked. She let out a little laugh. "You're not. I lied about the event starting at noon. It actually begins at half past 12."

Barry smiled. "You know me too well," he said with a laugh.

"And now you're right on time," Iris replied, kissing her husband's cheek. "They're starting the show!"

A young woman in a lab coat approached a podium, which had been set up in front of a giant black curtain. Barry knew her well. She was Janet Klyburn, the director of S.T.A.R. Labs.

"Welcome," Dr Klyburn announced. "We're so pleased to have you all here for this exhibition. Today's demonstration should be a fun way to show off five of our scientific advances. First, we have developed a fluorescent light source that glows with absolutely pure white light."

Barry glanced at the cannon-like metal tube in the middle of the room. On one side, a large lightbulb sat next to a giant triangular crystal. Between the crystal and the end of the tube was a circular screen.

"Next," said Dr Klyburn, "we developed a method of purifying quartz."

"This method created the flawless crystal prism you see here today," she continued. "The prism can turn white light into amazingly bright colours. The tube itself is able to keep these colours inside without energy loss, and yet doesn't overheat. Our fourth development is a triangle of three mirrors inside the tube. Each mirror is polished to absorb no light and reflect with extreme accuracy."

Barry nodded, impressed. None of the inventions was new, but each one was a scientific advancement.

"Our last development has exciting uses," Dr Klyburn said. "The whole system has been created to work as a projector, with unmatched brightness, clarity, and resolution. It revolutionizes the way we can project images anywhere!"

Dr Klyburn pressed a button on a remote control. **ZZRRRRRTT!** A mechanical shade suddenly blocked the skylight overhead, and the atrium dimmed.

"Ladies and gentlemen," she said, "I give you our King Kaleidoscope!"

Dr Klyburn pressed another button on the machine. **WHIR-WHIR-WHIR-WHIR!** The white circular screen rotated as the fluorescent light bulb flared. A beam of searing light sizzled into the prism. It shattered into a rainbow of vivid colours, which splashed onto the round screen.

Then the crystal began to rotate, swirling the colours on the screen. The kaleidoscope tube reflected the churning colours with its internal mirrors and projected them against the white ceiling. The audience oohed and ahhed.

Barry gasped at the kaleidoscope's stunning design overhead. The colours were incredible, brighter and crisper than any he'd ever seen. They whirled around on the ceiling. Then the colours broke into a pattern of triangles and spun in a brilliant mosaic circle.

Iris leaned against Barry, and he put his arm around her. They both gazed up in awe at the stunning light display.

A rainbow appeared, exploding through the centre of the display.

At first, Barry thought it was part of the show. Then, the end of the rainbow shimmered, and a solid object formed in the middle. A glowing man with goggles and a sleek costume appeared.

The evil man hovered in the air above the kaleidoscope and laughed nastily. "Welcome to my exhibition," he shouted, "of me taking over the world!"

"It's Rainbow Raider," Barry groaned.

CHAPTER 2

RAINBOW RAIDER

"What does he want?" Iris said as the audience gasped in alarm.

"What he always wants," Barry replied. "Power."

Rainbow Raider had pestered the Flash for years. Long ago, he had been an aspiring artist named Roy G. Bivolo. Unfortunately, Bivolo was born colour blind and had all his artwork rejected. Then one day, his dying father gave his son a pair of goggles that could control the colours of the rainbow.

The angered artist used the invention to start a life of crime. He attacked museums and other art-related places, but he soon desired even more power and wealth.

The goggles gave Rainbow Raider many amazing abilities. He could shoot solid beams of colour from his eyes or ride a rainbow through the air. The villain could also use colours to affect people's emotions or drain someone's colour to weaken them. Yet, Barry Allen had always thought of Rainbow Raider as a bother rather than a real menace.

"Are you going to stop him, or what?" Iris whispered to Barry.

"I already have," said the super hero with complete confidence.

Quicker than anyone in the crowd could see, Barry popped open the ring on his finger and released his compressed uniform. **PHWOOT!** He donned the suit faster than an eyeblink.

ZWWWOOOOMMMMM!

The Flash zipped and zagged through the atrium and leaped onto the tube of the kaleidoscope. "Clear out of here!" the hero told Rainbow Raider. "Why don't you leave before you get hurt?"

The crowd cheered at the appearance of their hometown hero.

"They cheer for you now," said the Rainbow Raider. "But when I'm done, the whole world will be chanting *my* name. They'll do what I tell them!"

A beam of blue light shot at the Flash.

The Flash tried to dodge out of the way, but he couldn't move faster than light.

KA-POW! The beam hit him right in the chest, and blue energy coursed through his body.

Suddenly, the super hero felt extremely sad. His shoulders slumped, and he felt exhausted by overwhelming misery. He had the blues.

The Flash didn't remember Rainbow Raider's colour powers being so strong before. Not that any thought mattered to him now. He was feeling so depressed that nothing seemed important.

Rainbow Raider laughed. "Now to finish you off," the villain said. His goggles glowed as he prepared to blast the Flash with another attack beam.

Oh, who cares? the Flash thought. The hero felt so miserable that he didn't even have enough energy to worry about being blasted.

But then, the Flash caught a glimpse of Iris in the crowd. She looked terribly worried for him. She cared. And the Flash cared for her deeply. He had no reason to be sad. He loved Iris, and she loved him.

With a super-speedy shiver, the Flash suddenly vibrated so quickly that he shimmied out of the blue energy. He left it behind like a shed skin.

This time, when Rainbow Raider released his attack beam, the Flash was ready for it. He leaped out of the way.

"I can't be bothered fighting you!" Rainbow Raider screeched. "I've got a world to conquer!" He dived towards the kaleidoscope's tube.

The Flash jumped into Rainbow Raider's path. He aimed a powerful punch right at the villain's face.

His fist rocketed through Rainbow Raider's head and came out the other side. The hero nearly fell over, pulled off balance as his punch hit nothing solid at all.

The Rainbow Raider was already gone. Flash had swung at nothing more than a vapour of colours left behind by the villain. The real Rainbow Raider was already making his getaway.

The Flash whirled around to see Rainbow Raider disappearing into the side of the kaleidoscope's tube. Immediately, the kaleidoscope's pattern on the ceiling began to whirl dizzyingly, growing bigger and bigger. *WHIR-WHIR-WHIR-WHIR!!*

The colours became brighter and more vibrant. They glowed with unearthly brilliance as Rainbow Raider added his powers to the kaleidoscope.

All the people in the audience gasped. They were dazzled by the swirling colours. Their mouths gaped open, and their eyes glazed over. The crowd all stood limp, hypnotized by the kaleidoscope's shimmering lights.

Don't look! the Flash warned himself. But the colours seemed to be everywhere, all around him, seeping into his mind.

Even after he squeezed his eyes shut, he could still see the swirling colours on the inside of his eyelids.

In seconds, the Flash was under Rainbow Raider's hypnotic control.

HYPNOTIZED!

"Do not fear," Rainbow Raider said. His voice echoed in the minds of his audience. "I will be a pleasant master. Most aspects of your lives will not change. The only difference is that I will rule you all."

The Flash tried to concentrate on escaping the hypnosis. The hero could think clearly but couldn't move his body. He couldn't even open his eyes.

How was Rainbow Raider going to take over the world if everyone could think but not move? the Flash wondered.

"When night falls, I will complete my plan," Rainbow Raider continued, his speech a sneering voice in everyone's mind. "I will project the kaleidoscope against the dark sky. Soon, the whole world will belong to me!"

Again, the Flash thought the super-villain's plan sounded half-baked. If the kaleidoscope's hypnotism only worked at night, everyone would be freed when the sun rose.

"I know what you must be thinking," Rainbow Raider's voice said from inside the kaleidoscope. "The hypnotism is effective in daytime – my colours will be there whether everyone can see them or not. But the first blast will have a more dramatic impact at night, when everyone can fully appreciate the most powerful artwork in history!"

The Flash's eyes ached from being squeezed shut. He tried to focus on his speed, willing himself to vibrate so that he could escape. But he couldn't move at all.

"Oh," the voice of Rainbow Raider said, "I suppose you're also wondering, 'How can we go about our tiny, boring lives if we can't move?' I simply wanted to show you the absolute control I have over you. Watch this demonstration. Don't speak! Don't escape! Don't move your feet! But now you can move the rest of your bodies."

Instantly, the Flash felt control return to his body – except for his feet, which he couldn't move at all. The hero opened his eyes. All around him, people were blinking their eyes and stretching their arms, but they remained rooted in place.

Nobody said a word.

The Flash glanced over at Iris. She looked terribly worried, and her gaze pleaded with him to stop the villain. The Flash couldn't let his wife down.

Rainbow Raider's head slid out of the kaleidoscope's top. He glared at everyone through his special goggles. When he spotted Flash looking at Iris, he smiled.

"Ah, my old enemy," the villain said. "You have feelings for that woman. How . . . interesting. Let's see how strong those feelings really are."

The Rainbow Raider slipped out of the kaleidoscope and landed next to Iris. "Does this bother you?" he asked the Flash.

The super hero tightened his hands into fists. He wanted to scream at Rainbow Raider, but he couldn't say anything.

The hero tried to zoom over to Iris's side, but his calf muscles only ached. He still couldn't move his feet.

"Look how angry you are!" Rainbow Raider told the Flash. "Let's see what I can add to that."

The villain shot a beam of green energy at the Flash.

The Flash felt his fury change to pure jealousy. Rainbow Raider was standing too close to Iris. The Flash's stomach churned. He seethed with suspicion. He gritted his teeth with murderous envy.

"How are you feeling?" Rainbow Raider asked. "You may speak now."

"I want . . . to destroy you!" the Flash spat out, unable to control his emotions.

"How delightful!" Rainbow Raider exclaimed. "Well, we can't let that happen. You should be afraid of me." The villain focused his goggles on the Flash again and blasted him with the yellow energy of cowardice.

The Flash shuddered with terror.

Rainbow Raider laughed. "Boo!" he said. "Are you feeling scared? Well, then, run! Run that way." He pointed towards the east. "As fast as you can!"

ZOOOM! Instantly, the Flash took off. He blazed through the wall of the atrium and cruised through the whole laboratory. When he was outside, the Flash picked up speed. He ran due east, vibrating through everything in his path.

In seconds, the Flash had broken the speed of sound. Lightning bolts of Speed Force crackled around him as he zoomed across the country. He was running so fast that his feet carried him across the surface of the ocean.

Still feeling jealous and fearful, the Flash zipped over the Atlantic in moments, and then blasted across Europe, Russia, and China. He passed Japan in a blur, and whipped across the waters of the Pacific.

Somewhere in the middle of the vast ocean, the super hero neared the speed of light. Suddenly, he pulled away from the energy of Rainbow Raider's colours. Shadows of green and yellow streamed along behind him. The jealousy and terror faded.

The Flash was so relieved to be free of those feelings that he almost tripped on the edge of North America. He quickly concentrated on his footing as he crossed the desert and headed over the Rocky Mountains. He'd be back in Central City in no time. He had to think of a plan – and fast.

Just then, an idea struck the hero like a lightning bolt. Rainbow Raider had told him to run towards the east. The villain hadn't actually said that he needed to go anywhere!

The Flash crossed the plains of the Midwest and zoomed through Keystone City. Then he blasted across the river to Central City.

Back at S.T.A.R. Labs, the Flash vibrated through the walls, running too fast for anyone to see him.

When he reached the kaleidoscope, he vibrated inside the tube. In the middle of the mirrored triangle, the super hero simply stopped moving forward. If he ran in place while facing east, the Flash wasn't disobeying Rainbow Raider.

The Flash's first thought was to break the mirrors, shutting down the kaleidoscope permanently.

WHODOOSH!

Still running in place, the hero glanced around to find the best place to attack. He spotted a strange sphere at the opposite end of the tube, where he couldn't reach it. The ball hovered outside the mirrored triangle, crackling with dark energy.

"A particle accelerator!" he said, gasping with surprise.

He had heard rumours that S.T.A.R. Labs had been working on such a device. It was supposed to speed up parts of atoms to create beams of high energy. These beams could be used for powerful X-ray machines and other scientific instruments.

Unfortunately, the energy could also be very unstable. In the wrong hands, it could trigger a nuclear explosion or even a black hole!

The Flash doubted that S.T.A.R. Labs had included a particle accelerator in their demonstration. Rainbow Raider must have hooked it up to the kaleidoscope to increase the power of his colours.

If the Flash destroyed the kaleidoscope while it was operating, he might trigger a reaction that would destroy Central City . . . and the entire solar system!

He had to shut down the machine safely. But how?

END OF THE RAINBOW

Rainbow Raider slid head-first into the kaleidoscope's tube. "You think you're hiding in here?" he asked the Flash. "Your blurred image is being projected onto the atrium's ceiling! You're ruining my artwork!"

His legs still pumping up and down, the Flash looked at the triangle of mirrors. His reflection was indeed scattered in the whirl of colours, repeated at weird, distorted angles. He was running so fast that his reflection was just a bright red shimmer.

The Flash grabbed his chance to attack Rainbow Raider. Running at nearly the speed of light, any movement the hero made could cause shock waves. He had to make a tiny, controlled movement that wouldn't damage the particle accelerator.

 The Flash simply snapped his fingers at Rainbow Raider and a burst of force slammed into the villain.

THWOOOOMMMMMM!!

Rainbow Raider didn't get knocked backwards as Flash expected. Instead, his body rippled like a pond into which someone had thrown a stone.

The villain wasn't made of flesh anymore. Strengthened by the device, the villain was nothing more than pure energy held together by his rainbow powers!

"Don't do that!" yelled Rainbow Raider.

The villain aimed his goggles at the Flash.

Rainbow Raider shot a rainbow beam out of his goggles at the super hero.

At the speed he was moving, the Flash dodged the rainbow blast easily.

The beam of rainbow-coloured force hit the floor of the mirrored triangle and reflected off the two angled top mirrors. The energy of the blast exploded throughout the tube.

The tube had been specially designed to keep energy inside. The high-powered beam sizzled around the hero and villain, gaining strength as it ricocheted from side to side.

The Flash was knocked off his feet. He hit the wall of the tube and fell onto the base mirror, his legs still running. **THUD!**

Then the hero heard an awful scream.

When Flash looked up, he saw Rainbow Raider being destroyed by his own blast.

Letting out another shriek, Rainbow Raider disintegrated. His particles spun wildly around the tube, joining all the other colours.

With all the extra energy growing inside the tube, the particle acceleration sphere glowed darker. Ominous streaks of black force arced around it.

The Flash stood. He had to stop the device before it turned into a black hole.

The sphere suddenly shrank, about to implode.

Now that he was free of Rainbow Raider's hypnotism, the Flash zoomed into action. There was only one way to calm the energy in the tube.

He had to cut off the light source.

In the split second before the sphere collapsed into a black hole, the Flash raced out of the end of the tube. He crashed into the fluorescent bulb, shattering it into millions of shards.

The colours on the ceiling also splintered into a million pieces. They fell to the ground like colourful raindrops.

The Flash held his breath, hoping he'd acted quickly enough to calm the particle accelerator.

A second passed. Then another.

The world was still in one piece.

The Flash let out a long sigh of relief. He'd been fast enough.

Now he just had to make sure no more light got into the kaleidoscope.

WHOOOOSH!

He raced over to the big black curtain behind the podium. He ripped it loose and then covered the whole tube with it.

The crowd in the atrium applauded.

The Flash rushed over to Iris and gave her a big hug. Then, smiling, he bowed to the cheering audience.

Dr Klyburn hurried over. "This wasn't supposed to happen!" she gasped.

The Flash nodded at her. "You'll find a stolen particle accelerator inside the tube," he said. "I doubt that was part of the original design."

Her eyes widened in alarm. "Of course not!" she assured him. "The kaleidoscope was under extremely tight security. Perhaps we failed to realize how dangerous this machine would be in the wrong hands."

"Don't blame the kaleidoscope," the Flash told her. "But maybe next time you should build in an easy-to-reach off switch!"

Iris squeezed the Flash's arm. "I don't think I'll ever enjoy looking at a rainbow again," she whispered.

The Flash smiled at his wife.

"Don't say that," he told her. "They're still beautiful. It was just our luck that instead of a pot of gold, this one had a villain at the end of it!"

RAINBOW RAIDER

REAL NAME: ROY G. BIVOLO

OCCUPATION: PROFESSIONAL CRIMINAL

HEIGHT: 1.78 METRES

WEIGHT: 75 KG

EYES: GREY

HAIR: BLACK

SPECIAL POWERS/ABILITIES:

High-tech goggles can shoot deadly hard-light projections, alter people's emotions with various coloured beams of light, and transport the villain from place to place.

done

RAINBOW RAIDER BIO

BIOGRAPHY:

From an early age, Roy G. Bivolo had wanted to be an artist. Unfortunately, Bivolo was born colour blind and his artwork was always rejected. Then one day, his dying father gave his son a pair of goggles that could control the colours of the rainbow. The angered artist used the invention to start a life of crime. He attacked museums and other art-related places, but he soon lusted for even more power and wealth. He joined the Rogues, a group of super-villains out to stop the Flash in his tracks.

RAINBOW RAIDER FACTS

Roy G. Bivolo's name contains the first letters of all the colours in the rainbow: **R**ed, **O**range, **Y**ellow, **G**reen, **B**lue, **I**ndigo, **V**iolet.

Rainbow Raider is a member of the Rogues Gallery. Other members include Captain Cold, Heatwave, Mirror Master, and Weather Wizard.

BIOGRAPHIES

J. E. Bright has had more than 50 novels, novelizations, and non-fiction books published for children and young adults. He is a full-time freelance writer, living in a tiny flat with his good, fat cat, Gladys, and his evil cat, Mabel, who is getting fatter.

Erik Doescher is a freelance illustrator and video game designer. He illustrated for a number of comic studios throughout the 1990s, and then moved into video game development and design. However, he has not given up on illustrating his favourite comic book characters.

Mike DeCarlo is a contributor of comic art whose range extends from Batman and Iron Man to Bugs Bunny and Scooby-Doo.

Lee Loughridge has been working in comics for more than fifteen years. He currently lives in a tent on the beach.

GLOSSARY

atrium patio or courtyard around which a building is built

exhibition public display of works of art, scientific advances, or other objects

hypnotize put someone in a trance

kaleidoscope tube that you twist and turn to view changing patterns made by coloured glass

mosaic pattern or picture made up of small pieces

prism a clear glass shape that bends light or breaks it up into different colours

quartz a hard mineral that comes in many different forms and colours

resentment feeling of being hurt or angered by something that has been done to you

resolution sharpness or clarity of an image

DISCUSSION QUESTIONS

1. Do you think Rainbow Raider's past might have caused him to become a super-villian? Why or why not?

2. The Flash uses his super-speed in many different ways. Discuss some of the ways Flash's unique superpower helped him in this story.

3. Rainbow Raider used his powers of colour to change the Flash's emotions. If you could choose one colour to describe yourself, what would it be? Explain your answer.

WRITING PROMPTS

1. Write another adventure about the Flash. What super-villain will he take on next time? How will he save the day?

2. Imagine you could run as fast as the Flash. Where would you go? What places would you see? Write about having super-speed for a day!

3. Create your own super hero. What superpowers does he or she have? What weaknesses? Write about your new super hero.